This book belongs to
_____

This book is dedicated to my children - Mikey, Kobe, and Jojo.

Copyright © 2024 by Grow Grit Press LLC. All rights reserved. No part of this book may be reproduced in any form without permission in writing from the publisher. Please send bulk order requests to info@ninjalifehacks.tv Printed and bound in the USA. MiniMovers.tv Paperback ISBN: 978-1-63731-907-9 Hardcover ISBN: 978-1-63731-909-3

Euclid

By Mary Nhin

Hi, I'm Euclid. I'm going to tell you a story about when I was younger like you! I loved asking questions and figuring out how things worked.

When I was young, growing up in Greece, I loved exploring the world around me. I collected rocks, built towers with sticks, and drew shapes in the sand.

One sunny day, I asked my teacher, "Why does a circle look different from a square?" My teacher smiled and said, "That's a wonderful question, Euclid! Let's find out together."

I loved going to school because it was full of answers to my many questions. But learning wasn't always easy. Sometimes, I got frustrated when I couldn't understand something right.

One morning, my teacher gave us a tricky puzzle. I tried and tried but couldn't solve it. I felt like giving up. But my teacher reminded me, "Euclid, every great mind faces challenges. Keep trying, and you'll find the answer."

With a lot of practice and patience, I started solving puzzles and understanding more about shapes and numbers. I learned about lines, circles, and angles.

Then one day, I realized that I could explain why a circle looks different from a square! I felt so proud. My teacher said, "Euclid, you have a gift for understanding geometry!"

I had many friends who loved to explore and learn with me. We would often sit together under the big, shady tree and share our discoveries.

We learned that working together and helping each other made learning even more fun. One of my favorite memories is when we built a giant sandcastle and measured all its sides and angles. It was like bringing my geometry lessons to life!

There were times when I failed to grasp new concepts, but I never gave up. I asked questions, practiced, and learned from my mistakes.

When I became an adult, I decided to write my own book to help others learn about geometry. I called it "Elements."

Writing the book was hard work. I had to be very patient and careful to explain everything clearly. Sometimes, I got tired and wanted to stop. But I remembered what my teacher had taught me: never give up and keep asking questions.

I kept writing and drawing shapes. I wanted everyone to understand geometry as well as I did.

Finally, my book "Elements" was finished! It was filled with everything I had learned about shapes, lines, and angles.

With my book, I traveled and taught many people about the wonders of geometry. People were excited to learn and thanked me for making geometry easier to understand. I felt happy knowing that I could help others with my work. It made all the hard work and challenges worth it.

As my friends and I grew older, we continued to explore new ideas and solve new puzzles. Our friendship and teamwork made us strong. I hope you have friends to learn and explore with, too. Together, you can achieve wonderful things.

My challenges taught me to be patient and persistent. My successes showed me the joy of discovery.

So, if you ever face a challenge, don't give up. Keep asking questions and exploring the world around you.

Timeline

Circa 330 BCE – Euclid is born.

Circa 300 BCE – Euclid begins teaching at the Library of Alexandria, Egypt.

Circa 300 BCE – Euclid compiles his most famous work, Elements.

Post 300 BCE – Euclid writes other significant mathematical and scientific texts.

I love hearing from my readers.
Write to me at info@ninjalifehacks.tv or send mail to:

Mary Nhin
5 West 15th St.
Edmond, OK 73013

Visit NinjaLifeHacks.tv for lesson plans and more!

 @marynhin   @officialninjalifehacks    Ninja Life Hacks
#minimoversandshakers

 Mary Nhin   Ninja Life Hacks    @officialninjalifehacks

www.ingramcontent.com/pod-product-compliance
Lightning Source LLC
Chambersburg PA
CBHW042147200426
43209CB00066B/1810